Whatever we see is changing, losing its balance. The reason everything looks beautiful is because it is out of balance, but its background is always in perfect harmony. This is how everything exists in the realm of Buddha nature, losing its balance against a background of perfect balance. So if you see things without realizing the background of Buddha nature, everything appears to be in the form of suffering. But if you understand the background of existence, you realize that suffering itself is how we live, and how we extend our life.

Shunryu Suzuki, ***Zen Mind, Beginner's Mind***

THE BLADE OF MANJUSRI

Poems by Neil Myers

Sun Moon Bear Editions, Geyserville, California

The Blade Of Manjusri copyright © Neil Myers, 1989. All rights reserved. Printed in the United States of America.

This first edition of **The Blade Of Manjusri** published in 1989 by Sun Moon Bear Editions, 17807 Lytton Station Road, Geyserville, California 95441

ACKNOWLEDGMENTS

Cover photo by Vern Cheek.
Photo of Mr. Myers by Natalie Leimkuhler.

"Two For O'Keeffe" and "Homage To The *Tao Te Ching*" first appeared in *The Chariton Review*.

The epigraph is from Shunryu Suzuki, *Zen Mind, Beginner's Mind*, paperback ed., 32 (Tokyo: John Weatherhill, 1985) by permission of Tanko-Weatherhill, Inc. The quotation on page 40 is reprinted from *Samadhi* by Mike Sayama, by permission of the State University of New York Press, © 1986, State University of New York.

Many thanks to the Purdue University School of Liberal Arts whose Center for Creative Endeavors Fellowship allowed me to write this book. Warm gratitude also to Lee Perron, for his companionship in poetry over the years. A deep gassho to Sekiun Koretsune, beloved sensai, of Kyoto, as well as to the sangha of the Minnesota Zen Meditation Center and the teachers I met at Hokyoji, Dainin Katagiri and Tozen Akiyama, for their generosity and nurturing strength.

ISBN 0-9620634-1-X paper edition
ISBN 0-9620634-2-8 cloth edition
Library of Congress Catalog Card Number 89-63056

for Lorna, Rachel & Julie

The Blade Of Manjusri

1

I want only to look
at the letters
containing the faces of God

which are the faces of death
& not death itself

life is there too
in the features
& a thousand things running
in a thousand directions

as if
I could hold
my hand up & ask them to sit
& contemplate themselves

which I do
now

2

Perhaps to write
about the faces of God
is always to lie

That must be true
the letters swirl & writhe
go misty smoky
threaten to melt

but they're all we have

or is that true?

It must be
They're all we have
to melt
before the letters of the name
of God

which is a name
for something else

3

The letters that compose
the presence of God
that bind it
& seal it in a web
all these sentences
clumsy rhythms
junctures pictures
moments
silences

also live
in the dark shadows
on which
an angel floats
holding a sword
cutting us off

from present from future & past
from our tongues
& all they have said

& whatever they're going to say
to you & you & you
now

4

God of our kneecaps eyeballs tendons
skin shirt hair

without Whom there would be none of these things
& no dead
who also revered You
& made You live

without Whom we would have no hands
& couldn't open anything

water would run over us
like turtle shells or sea stones
pearly glistening
white as marrowless bone

without You
nothing would follow
or come before

only air
vibrating in lungs
heads turning
flowers blooming
white yellow red
year by year

5

I need to add my name
to the sound of a distant hammer
beating at the horizon
its flat brass
going perpetually
days now

years maybe

over & over
like artificial thunder
stage set storms

never rising or falling in volume
& maybe I'm the only one listening
& have been for days

years

therefore I want to give it my name
height weight eye color
shadowing

which will vibrate
along with all

silence
before the crash
& after

6

One remembers solely
the clarity of final things

all forms are empty painful real
are viable reasonable visible
answerable by death & change

even in late age
perhaps a moment of discovery
of burial in the here
a long cleft a diamond a sliver
enters the flesh
& gleams there

o anger fear irritability
o the ragged edge of this supreme universe
o the small tatters we hold in our hands
as we lunge to the end of our leashes

7

a stupor a wild skid
a long sigh from the
nearest bushes katy-
dids a muffled clash
across a metal roof
a dark angel ready to
select whatever is

8

In attachment to any form is anguish.
Then
in release from any attachment to any form
is the release from anguish.

Release thru the body of anguish.

Anguish & release are one.

You must sit & fold your hands
& be in the universe of anguish

flowering in anguish.

You must be what you are, a flower of anguish.

Anguish so extreme it is abstract
like a flag
an overwhelming rippling weave of anguish

hillsides breathing anguish
buckling below you

saying, you have failed, failed, your failure is the body
  of anguish, the seed & the husk

from this there is no release

except

in the body of anguish itself

in the darkness of the husk

the flowering seed

do not be afraid

of the body of anguish
& its release

9

O follower

of fear
& compassion

the deep veins
of zazen

the surface grasses
waving

the fear of ghosts & demons
furious dancers

mind waves
still mind

the 2 one

Note: Manjusri is a meditating bodhisattva of compassion often portrayed with a fierce expression, and with a sword that separates the illusory from the real.

Love Poem

Sky one morning over a New Mexico gulley,
pinyon, mesquite, a distant river over rocks,
small birds settling once something large has passed,
your face so close it could be an element.
I can see all that clearly now, & past.
Sometimes I can't.

Summer, Late

& a cardinal begins in the far yard,
under the rainy stems, the cities of leaves,
a looping wheeper whee whu
that pulls my body back
from its long contract with anguish & death.
I can see cardinals out here often,
on chairs, in snow, against scattered cans & drab grass,
& perhaps that's what Katagiri meant
("there is also deep joy!")
when I said I saw awakening as grief,
the soul going on going off like a match,
flash.

Sounding

A jay flings over the lawn three stories down.
I'm ready for anything.
When I look again, light has hung metal on the trees,
motors whir, the house sinks lightly in the haze,
& sings of desolation, as trough calls to trough
    in violent seas.
I'm washed by waves, sand fills my mouth, the dead
    are near, I clutch pebbles,
& want to talk without resolving anything,
continuously.

•

Gradually, deliberately, I'm taking
what I trust of the earth & holding it to my face,
tasting its odd moisture, letting it go.
I've been doing this for years,
but now I'm aware of it,
& of the way my hand opens to scatter small clods,
dust spurs, root webs, beetle shells
toward the ground below my feet, in the light dusk,
again, again.

•

Small black fruits have appeared overnight in
    the yellowing hackberry,
tiny periods among the stems.
Soon the waxwings will arrive, unabashed & restless,
with their steel gray stomachs & dark hoods,

flitting, winking, chewing testily.
A few bees slice at the window & curve off
    in damaged hooks.
I wave at dust rings, which whirl, pile & hug
like bodies reconditioned at Pompeii,
dense textured, cinder clean, fists tangled,
    knees to mouth.

•

Trees raise their branches.
They have something to say about exposure,
abandoning everything, feeling, shape of skull,
to the space between veins where it is getting colder.
What good to be thin as paper?
Like answering a phone in endless panic
or just being rocked for years above pavings & roofs,
under clouds,
their dark scrolls unrolling, translating,
whose print we are.

Fall Piece

A finch suddenly aims toward the window & away,
a yellow green black blur,
& surfacing past it all morning, in sunny haze,
the shapes, barriers, tubes, twigs, knobs, stars, hubs
of a million universes in dirt & bark,
thumb-lives, speck-lives, knuckle-lives,
wadded, tasted on tongues, spat from mouths & holes.

O the potato sized shell of this world
& the elements standing on it,
arms out, heads up, wings shining & jiggling,
eyes if any high-stalked, clear, frowning.

Heat is vanishing.
It may freeze tonight.

O world of innumerable satiations & insufficiencies.
& my iron thumb
that has never made anything grow very well,
    indoors or out.

I see now it's made little difference.
O my iron thumb.

Sandhills, October

To see the world without distress
& with generalizations large enough
to fall steadily
like cranes dropping a field's length
past this rail
where your hand now rests

& even those usually dissatisfied
& feeling mistreated
staring in deep surprise
at this intricacy of sky, ground & season,
its wings held out & back, its persistence.

Fall Piece

A finch suddenly aims toward the window & away,
a yellow green black blur,
& surfacing past it all morning, in sunny haze,
the shapes, barriers, tubes, twigs, knobs, stars, hubs
of a million universes in dirt & bark,
thumb-lives, speck-lives, knuckle-lives,
wadded, tasted on tongues, spat from mouths & holes.

O the potato sized shell of this world
& the clements standing on it,
arms out, heads up, wings shining & jiggling,
eyes if any high-stalked, clear, frowning.

Heat is vanishing.
It may freeze tonight.

O world of innumerable satiations & insufficiencies.
& my iron thumb
that has never made anything grow very well,
    indoors or out.

I see now it's made little difference.
O my iron thumb.

Sandhills, October

To see the world without distress
& with generalizations large enough
to fall steadily
like cranes dropping a field's length
past this rail
where your hand now rests

& even those usually dissatisfied
& feeling mistreated
staring in deep surprise
at this intricacy of sky, ground & season,
its wings held out & back, its persistence.

Riddles

The puzzle I'm trying to solve
has to do with ideas

of emptiness, or falling
into warm places in a cold current,

or cold in a warm,
& keeping my arms out

to pray or protect myself.
The difficulty

lies in interpreting messages
like sleep, eat,

drive, breathe,
be elemental, go with the flow,

walk on water, leave things alone,
respect their terrible travail

as they move with you,
keep your consciousness clear

for what you trust,
carry it as far as you can,

know what's behind you,
& ahead & beside you .

go

Exile

At any moment
you can move to any other moment

or space
sit under a tree

in sun or spotted shadow
completely absorbed

& forgetful
& if others speak to you

ignore them
or compose scenes

that stand behind you
by decades

that's exile
& whoever demanded it

must be leaning over you
asking you to wake up

that's the spirit of exile
that you forget

as you rise
in astonishment

like a cat
starting to lap milk

with its tongue .

Bricolage

Let things lie
where they've fallen
scattered on my desk,

prospectus & envelope,
Castle & Cooke
(sign & mail),

& a smooth, pink brown
fist sized
grinding stone

plucked from a mesa
at Ojo Caliente,
easily 800 years old,

& past it a glossy
chip of an
arrowhead, thousands

strewn in the dirt
& shards, o love,
love, I draw a lung-

full of panic & hope,
& ease it out
of a deep shaft

on a dry rope.

Herman Hesse Reading Hate Mail From Germany At The Beginning Of The First World War

The fly at the fringes of his arm flicks harmlessly.
Someone is chattering.
White fungi line damp logs by the door.
Dark spots cluster on his thumb.
It rains in puffs.
Smoke unrolls slow worms.
A dozen figures cringe near the floor.
Some he abandoned, some he couldn't bear.
Together they'll climb fire-steps.
All loneliness is guilt.
Europe is hair & ash.
It will be to himself when he talks again, quietly.

Tamino In The Cave Of Terror

He's trying to tell the children, *sing
deliberately, sing of order,* but
the piece runs from his mouth, the tune
leaks, speeds around the stage like
a fizzling balloon. He wants to hear
something else, but before he can start
one of the sympathetic ones jumps up &
tears the score from his hand, & races
off, scattering it, so fragments,
spindly bits & ashes, float toward
the wings where air is drifting in.
What more do you want, he screams, but
they've vanished, & in their places
demons, bent & hairy, & angels, eyes
rimmed gold, heads blue, are warning
him to keep off, keep divesting himself
until his soul becomes what it needs
to be, a small hard knot, walnut warm,
& intricate as treasure. For years,
he thinks, he's stumbled this way, only
to discover this. The journey's been
for this. He could have arrived
years earlier, but so much to burn away.

Papageno Going South

Here is the motive for climbing into old
slants of sun, along the lower branches,
where he hangs & shivers, snapping at berries,
pulsing, since nothing can happen until
veins warm, wings tingle, lice dissolve,
& he rises, astonished, stem by stem, across
blind space, faster & colder than anything
he dreamed of in the country where he first
saw greenery, buds, bugs, faces -- O this
eggshell world, finally he's figured how
to let it go, whatever it is, or wants
him to be, whatever he will be, or just was.

TWO FOR O'KEEFFE

1 Pelvis With Moon

> "The abstraction is often the most definite form
> for the intangible thing in myself that I can only
> clarify or paint."

It must be something she's noticed half
a valley away, for months -- an intractable
clear lump, exposed beside some common
rise or track, an eye of blue within a pearl.
Tho when she reaches it, it's gone,
vanished under boulders, roots, dead stumps.
So she knows she has to continue, thrusting
into distance, straddling forms,
delivering them out. Probing. Homing.

All day, nothing. This must be accurate, she
thinks, this furious drifting, signs
that mark the site with absence, *Slow*,
Pass. It is no dream. Hills are whitening,
leaves thinning, vast shelves of sage,
puffs of nuthatch, waxwing. When crows
arrive they take her in their mouths, &
spit her, miles off. The place is vacant,
like the end of anything. Wind or
concentration. Circles. Apertures. Height. Touch.

Or like the sounds the most intimate shapes
make taking cues from whatever's at hand :

the way nails scrape, & fold up from
inside, or how, at the farthest rim,
stars break, lights dip, smoke stirs,
*no need to realize anything but what
they said you couldn't bear.* How many years
has she known that? She stares, startled, as if
the thing looked back, & uttered all
it saw: this scale & ground, bone-clean.   *Here.*

2 Ram's Skull

> "I am often amazed at the spoken and written word telling me what I have painted . . . . no one else can know how my paintings happen."

She's spent the morning putting things
aside, & framing views, of doors,
arroyos, roads silvering toward gravel.
She studies distant textures, how wind
flays cliffs like templates, cuts
a mesa. In a tree new shadows. Focus
in drifts & petals. It thunders at her.

She's bored. She checks a window. It's
bright, buds spill at crazy angles,
glass leaves, a bullsnake looping up
the scrub to butt a house, warm rock,
blank shed. She lets a fist uncurl
& flicks a horn, deep hull & whorl. *Tap.
Tap.* Outside? It may be speaking in her.

Forgettings. Long delays. Dogs roaming
in them, somewhere past the socket,
toward the jaw. Late yellow in the
half light at the nostril. When she
reaches it, it whisks off, chattering,
trembling to attention, depth & shape.
Whatever she's figured on, for months.

Horizons, stems, a way. The rest predictable.

Homage To The *Tao Te Ching*

The five colors blind the eye.

All week I hear birds burst among the
backyard leaves: stars, splits, pinwheels,
plugs, rachets, rips, slides, specks.
It's endless, quick. Ten thousand scales
wink wildly, asking that we all be
harmless from now on; tho if we never lived
the rest would be intact, sunk in the world's
crotch like a knife in a pig's neck.
Or maybe we're not really at war with
everything that spills us, in crowds of
rainbows, clucks & flares. Maybe it's
as it should be. Scarred. Flawed. Blurred.

2 Ram's Skull

> "I am often amazed at the spoken and written word
> telling me what I have painted . . . . no one else can
> know how my paintings happen."

She's spent the morning putting things
aside, & framing views, of doors,
arroyos, roads silvering toward gravel.
She studies distant textures, how wind
flays cliffs like templates, cuts
a mesa. In a tree new shadows. Focus
in drifts & petals. It thunders at her.

She's bored. She checks a window. It's
bright, buds spill at crazy angles,
glass leaves, a bullsnake looping up
the scrub to butt a house, warm rock,
blank shed. She lets a fist uncurl
& flicks a horn, deep hull & whorl. *Tap.*
Tap. Outside? It may be speaking in her.

Forgettings. Long delays. Dogs roaming
in them, somewhere past the socket,
toward the jaw. Late yellow in the
half light at the nostril. When she
reaches it, it whisks off, chattering,
trembling to attention, depth & shape.
Whatever she's figured on, for months.

Horizons, stems, a way. The rest predictable.

Homage To The *Tao Te Ching*

The five colors blind the eye.

All week I hear birds burst among the
backyard leaves: stars, splits, pinwheels,
plugs, rachets, rips, slides, specks.
It's endless, quick. Ten thousand scales
wink wildly, asking that we all be
harmless from now on; tho if we never lived
the rest would be intact, sunk in the world's
crotch like a knife in a pig's neck.
Or maybe we're not really at war with
everything that spills us, in crowds of
rainbows, clucks & flares. Maybe it's
as it should be. Scarred. Flawed. Blurred.

Those who do not know awe are near catastrophe.

Their margins thick against the snow,
trees, waiting for their lives to start
over. Dusk, distant & heavy. They stretch
out slowly, across the foreign sky. How
did this happen? How did they arrive?
Here's night, & lovely cold, the deep
lustres of its outlines, pores & nostrils,
hairs that reach up toward a house
where flames reflect our faces at them.
Bruegel, someone says, high whites
with blackened slabs, *like Bruegel.*
As if that could be an answer.
A reference point. An angle from a window.

The sage never tries to store things up.

The pleasure of throwing out opens me
to things without clear purpose again:
two cats a fence away, one craftily
shadowing the other; the nutty dog next
door, terrorizing fantastic interlopers,
doves huddled near a hedge, clouds
answering clouds. I mean, most stuff
lets up some time in its own way, & that's
the joy: the graver the cut the farther
it extends, until just sky is left,
& cans, skins, shards, shells, small flakes
of bones, a trash-lipped rim of grass.

The still is the master of unrest.

Fog. Backyard sparrows. Suppose that nothing's
over, the whole scene floated up
from where it just peeled off, a million
lunky branches waving freely when
a squirrel slam-dunks the web. I take
a breath, & see, *I'm here, & in the clear,*
across one contour, a sort of edge whose
surface is exposed, & bare, & curved,
& things are different from what I think
I've said. A tune unexpected. & now
it steps out. A tall figure, a far-off
tower of clouds? I squint. A clump of woods?

Better stop short than fill to the brim.

I'm staying quiet, fixed on the linchpin
of my life, & nothing's moving me except
the sudden realization, *all there is*.
Like a stone falling for years, & hitting
somewhere soft. The morning perfect,
cool, threaded across the thinning leaves,
abandoned intimacies of sleep, an urge
to let things mean, thru focus, time & sun.
Just weather, helping them along. Seeing
a shade, & hearing less & less: wind,
the pounding, swelling of my breath, & blood.

Discretions

If it's panic you've chosen to carry,
give it weight,
it'll keep you grounded, under wild confusion
& the terrible birds that croak around you.
Give it voice. Walk away.

•

Mind raps its damp skull on a trunk.
Things happen one by one.
Boom.
Explosions of clouds, sun on suddenly cool greenery,
& in the park this morning, thru the trees,
an astonishing sight, a heron, wings just visible,
flapping hugely off, a flick of long white
slowly gaining altitude in seconds.
Boom. Boom.

•

Stick your arm in water
& your hand bends at the wrist.
Bring it out & it is straightened.
Hold it up & it is dripping.
It may be weeping when you straighten again.

•

Cancel your wisdom.
Merge it in the drying leaves, the grass lipping toward
    the whitened earth,
the pulse of these lines,
the mild machine-heat under your fingers,
the sides of your hands resting on tingling metal,
friends gathering prayers, as you gathered theirs,
over your own death, so vague,
& your dead, blinding, profuse, preposterous.

       •

The unexamined life is worth nothing,
except to the sleeper who pulls it thru an alley
where examined things lie rusting.

       •

Sit down, alone, in the darkening hours.
If others have little, you have less & less.
Stare thru deep cold at first stars, snow bands on roofs,
    trivia falling in a fine dust.
A stillness sweeps on when you least expect.

Little Soul

Does your last breath rest somewhere on a cushion
    of air?
Will others inhale it too?

& that pumping in your chest
is that God
telling his angels not to applaud, not yet?

Quick Fix

In the universe of spiders
a single web

in the single web of the universe
the spiders

one spider
in the single web of the universe

one spider
one web

Jahrzeit For My Father

I swim among old words
like a cripple scrambling for a cane,
bewildered by the short space between fingers & wall,
table glass & candle glass,
& my own voice angling
past the cliches I use to mourn --
diamonds on my palm, rainbows in a window.

I Keep Hearing A Fan Swirl

& the flap of sparrows in the billion towers of leaves,
handfuls, mouthfuls, shelves, fountains, riddles,
scenes I want to see again before I fall,
gripping the solid round under my claws,
& hearing the darkness peck against the shadows filling
under my beak.

Mind Waves/Game Plan

In my confusion
I can barely absorb
the simplest thing

to let the mind
be the most confused
simplest thing

& let confusion be
the simplest thing
since the simplest

thing in my con-
fusion is to
let confusion be

Hakuin

> "One evening while Shoju was cooling himself on a veranda, Hakuin presented a verse. 'Delusions and fancies,' Shoju said. Hakuin shouted back, 'Delussions and fancies!' Shoju seized him, rained twenty or thirty blows on him, and pushed him off the veranda."
>
> Mike Sayama, *Samadhi*

O zazen. Wind blows
on the steps of afternoon thunder.

I reach for a slot to drop
pain, & feel it bunch & disperse

then knit together again.
I stop, knowing I always can

stop further. Yesterday a tornado 40 miles north
demolished a trailer,

knocked a dozen homes & several people about,
lifted a man out of his kitchen & threw him

against a shed, lifted a garage with
a car but left the car intact

& the woman in it. Today in the half
dark of midday the trunks look

blanker & plainer than ever.
I can see their detailed

cracks & layerings & borings & ridges.
Whatever is necessary is here, here

where it has always been. Shoju to Hakuin
& his desperation, "Dead monk in a cave,"

shoving him in the mud, where he lay
face down. I have fallen between

labor & labor. I blink, shake, look up.
Rain is approaching, air like a vice.

Thru a patch of highest stems
the sky is turning. I can forget the rest.

I can forget the need for blessing.
What do you want, says a voice.

I can clap & exhale.
I can begin by laughing.

Casually

is how things start, & end, rarely
as expected, tho a brief juncture
often joins them at the middle. Like
now. I'm upstairs, listening to my
wife & daughter talk about clothing
in quick snippets, & staring down-
yard, at the brilliant chokeberries
in the deep green rags of bushes.
Focus & relax, I think, the rest takes
care of itself, tho in detail it's
unpredictable: the slipslap of a heli-
copter that just buzzed the house,
then our stunned alertness, then my
urge to be exact, about the power of
red, in veins, dots, flowers, slashes,
sky, time, place, where lives keep
racing at their own calm pace,
ineptitude, or savage brittleness.

Summer Group, Long Island (after a painting by Alex Katz)

They may be dreaming the whole thing,
the channel buoy swinging, the boat

bobbing & tipping, the sail ready to
descend, the bowsprit's whoof flap

slap. Heat, weeds, shells, scales
tonguing odd folds of skin, moths

furious on screens, unimpassioned
spiders, trees khaki-dry & mushroom

pale. That's how it happens, floods
of weather wrinkling the charts, the

way they lean toward each other under
pressure, pleasure, grief, lucky to

witness every instant, to survive
by whim, charm, all of the above.

Alpine Scene, for Lorna

Mountain from our window,
fir lines, dense ridges,
black
        road,
                2 stars in
water,
        snow.
                      The rest is
absence, that holds most
things together,
                tho what
we love is streaked with
what we lack.
                Between 2
deaths our lives take
clumsy shape,
              3 peaks
rising,

        lake.

Letters

If there are tongues there are yellow flowers
wires continue clouds & openings
where am I going

When I stop the pip
birds insects meet the smell of heat on metal
grass

I hold your small book in my hand
reattached to my arms
nothing moves in the valley of waste

Small waves grey light
surf sandstrip cursive with prints
a motionless rush

A huge iron breath
birds hills earthweave
a flat palm waving not I greet you but Storm

Words shreds burning
grey blue smoke
rope into the unachievable past

Quiet & the night's double needle
to lie still
let stillness talk

Two Mysteries

Let things go out of control
Let things be orderly

One Mystery

Let things out of control
be orderly

Another Mystery

Order things
out of control

A Form of Control

Order things
into a mystery

A Form of Disorder

The mystery of things
out of control

Order

Let things be out of control
Let things be mysteries

Cicadas

As if a wire had snapped, & the whole swarm plunged thru
    the clumsy dark,
shearing the weeds, the little umbrellas of the stems,
wrapped in horny circuits, up & back & back,
the storms of haunches sawing near us,
inside & around us, in goiters, hinges, throats.

      •

I'm ready for anything.
The climate hasn't changed.
When I call a chipper voice tells me the time, the
    humidity, the latest high-low.
I run my tongue over the sea ridges of my palate,
tasting warty flesh & teeth like fine flames.
Everything's in place, smeared with generosity & growth.

      •

Sometimes the horizon narrows to a closet's length,
where walls peel, hangers rattle, & an insect
stirs a memory of dusty coats,
their high-domed collars, their camphorous folds,
ready for seasons that have long since worn them,
leaving spotted flesh,
while it continues,
the only creature in the universe without light, or rest.

Radii

I hold two candles, one in each hand.
Each day I blow one out, the other is renewed.
As for my mind, it has its potholes & dead ends.
Daily a postman seeks an address there,
& finds my father's lovely face, my brother's height,
  my children's outstretched palms.
We're all diverse, but he can recognize us by our
  fates & flaws,
& the radiance thrown by the candles, one glowing
  incessantly,
out of the central void I'm walking from.

O Zazen

Send awareness out
in a circle
of hands & arms

•

On the rim between
failure
& breath

•

Halves of lightning
meeting
heaven & earth

•

Week after week
staring at the rough cedar
of my will

•

The mouse of the throat
warbling
still here!

•

Noise filled &
noiseless
I reach toward a shore

•

Rimmed in chaos
a dark
morning hangs ahead

•

Incessantly not
knowing
again & again

•

Katydids
low shrill
skins of weeds & trees

•

O irritability
the ragged
edges of the world

•

For 40 minutes
no change
everything the same

•

Always
uttering the world
let the stone fall

•

Tiny wing
pinched gonad
shriveled seed

•

A sudden gust
may shake it down
something must

•

The original
I/you
to appease

•

My father in his chair
legs swollen arms out
"my mind never stops"

•

Here
in my palm
it is beating now

•

Susceptible
as never before
to love & grief

•

Like a hand held up
the lovely
yellowing leaves

•

Her voice
frail with cigarettes
& beginnings

•

Returning to
flame
it can't flee any more

•

A long sigh
from the nearest bushes
katydids

•

Stone ball
carying sunlight
meteor pocks

•

All's well
because
it has to be

•

In the circle of the dead
my own
unceasing breath

•

Suddenly a small leaf
yellower
than the rest

History

First there was panic
then waking up.
West, north, I see
what I love,
rolling thunderheads,
a gauze of fields,
a stitching of brief light.
Dry sticks.
The earth can burn with what is real.

A poet widely published in magazines, Neil Myers is the author of *All That, So Simple* (Purude University Press, 1980) and a chapbook, *Tippecanoe* (1972). He lives in West Lafayette, Indiana, where he teaches English and Creative Writing at Purdue University. His work is shaped by a long-standing involvement with Zen Buddhism. He writes, "A poem is a constant chipping away at the rock of confusion. For me, at the moment, the lovely discipline of zen meditation (zazen) is the hammer in my hand."

The Blade of Manjusri, published in the fall of 1989, 50 numbered copies bound in boards by the Earle Gray Bindery and signed by the author. 300 copies in paper wraps. Prepress, MMT. Thanks to Jeffrey Miller & Tim Owens for graphic consultation. Book design by Lee Perron. Printed at Mariner Graphics on Mohawk Superfine paper in 11 pt. Trump Mediaeval typeface and produced peripatetically in West Lafayette, Indiana, Los Angeles, & Healdsburg, California.